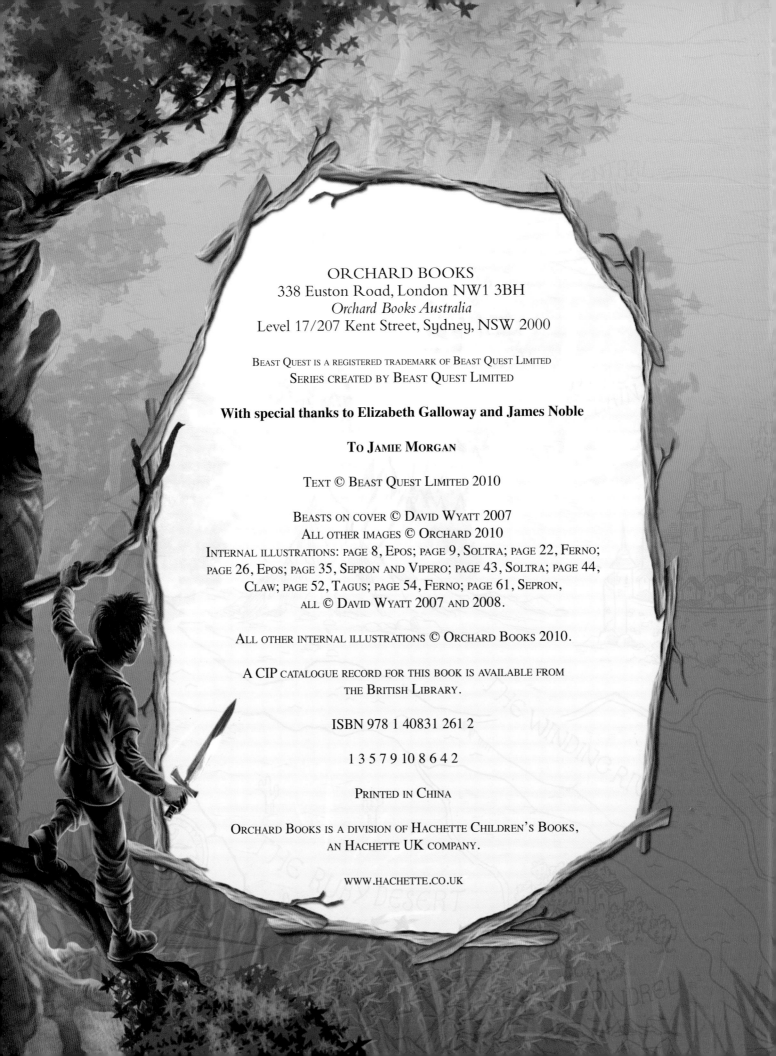

ORCHARD BOOKS
338 Euston Road, London NW1 3BH
Orchard Books Australia
Level 17/207 Kent Street, Sydney, NSW 2000

BEAST QUEST IS A REGISTERED TRADEMARK OF BEAST QUEST LIMITED
SERIES CREATED BY BEAST QUEST LIMITED

With special thanks to Elizabeth Galloway and James Noble

TO JAMIE MORGAN

TEXT © BEAST QUEST LIMITED 2010

BEASTS ON COVER © DAVID WYATT 2007
ALL OTHER IMAGES © ORCHARD 2010
INTERNAL ILLUSTRATIONS: PAGE 8, EPOS; PAGE 9, SOLTRA; PAGE 22, FERNO;
PAGE 26, EPOS; PAGE 35, SEPRON AND VIPERO; PAGE 43, SOLTRA; PAGE 44,
CLAW; PAGE 52, TAGUS; PAGE 54, FERNO; PAGE 61, SEPRON,
ALL © DAVID WYATT 2007 AND 2008.

ALL OTHER INTERNAL ILLUSTRATIONS © ORCHARD BOOKS 2010.

ISBN 978 1 40831 261 2

1 3 5 7 9 10 8 6 4 2

PRINTED IN CHINA

ORCHARD BOOKS IS A DIVISION OF HACHETTE CHILDREN'S BOOKS,
AN HACHETTE UK COMPANY.

WWW.HACHETTE.CO.UK

ANNUAL 2011

This book belongs to

....

Contents

Welcome, followers of the Quest!

In this annual, you will learn about my battle to free the Kingdom of Avantia from the evil of Wizard Malvel. I have released Good Beasts from his spells, battled wicked Beasts, and travelled through strange and terrifying realms.

Now it is time for YOUR Beast Quest. Malvel has hidden six magical tokens among the pages of this book.

Can you spot them all? You will discover their importance later…

Your Quest will lead you to fiendish games, quizzes and activities that will test your skill and bravery. Along the way, you'll meet great friends – but also fearsome enemies.

Destiny and danger await. Keep a sword by your side and courage in your heart.

Good luck, my friend…

Tom

TOM

The bravest boy in Avantia. He seeks no glory, and only wishes to keep the kingdom safe from evil. Tom does not back down from any challenge, and will follow his Beast Quests wherever they take him.

EPOS

The oldest Beast in the kingdom, Epos is the guardian of the Stonewin Volcano. Her two great powers are immortality – when she dies, she is reborn, stronger than ever – and creating fireballs.

THE QUEST BEGINS

In Errinel, a village in Avantia, a boy called Tom lived with his Aunt Maria and Uncle Henry, a blacksmith. Tom dreamed of finding his long-lost father, Taladon, and having great adventures.

One day, Errinel's crops were destroyed by mysterious fires. Henry declared that someone had to ask for King Hugo's help. Tom eagerly volunteered. He sneaked into the palace and heard the king talking about how a knight had been killed by a dragon!

Tom volunteered to challenge the dragon. The Good Wizard Aduro saw that Tom was a courageous boy – and the son of Avantia's greatest warrior, Taladon. Aduro assured the king that Tom might be Avantia's saviour. The king gave Tom his blessing.

Armed with a sword, shield and a stallion called Storm, Tom's Beast Quest began!

On his journey, Tom came across a girl and her wolf, being chased by soldiers. Tom saved her life, and gained two loyal friends: Elenna and Silver. Together, they fought and defeated Ferno the Fire-Dragon, and five other Beasts that had been bewitched by Aduro's great enemy, the dark wizard Malvel.

THE GOLDEN ARMOUR

Malvel wanted revenge, so he stole a precious Avantian artefact, the Golden Armour. It belonged to Tom's missing father, Taladon. Malvel scattered the six pieces across Avantia, and set six evil Beasts to guard them. But Tom was up to the challenge of getting the armour back.

On this Quest, Tom and Elenna travelled the kingdom again, discovering new regions and villages. They had to defeat Zepha the Monster Squid, Claw the Giant Monkey, Soltra the Stone Charmer, Vipero the Snake-Man, and Arachnid the King of Spiders.

Finally, their Beast Quest took them to the Central Plains, where they challenged Malvel's fiercest Beast yet – Trillion the Three-Headed Lion.

After conquering each evil Beast, Tom gained a new piece of the Golden Armour – and new magical gifts that made him more powerful than ever.

ELENNA

Tom's best friend is Elenna, a girl from the south-west of Avantia. Plucky and resourceful, Elenna has saved Tom's life many times. He could not survive his Beast Quests without her.

SOLTRA

One of Tom's toughest Beast Quests was against Soltra the Stone Charmer. She lured people with her beautiful voice – but one glance at her single eye turned her victims to stone. Soltra stalked the marshlands beside Tom's beloved home village – Errinel.

THE DARK REALM

In Gorgonia, beneath a terrifying red sky, Tom and Elenna faced Malvel's most evil Beasts yet. But defeating them was not the only goal on this new Beast Quest. Malvel had lured the Good Beasts of Avantia to the Dark Realm, and they were his prisoners!

On this Quest, Tom had to face Torgor the Minotaur, Skor the Winged Stallion (who was ridden by Malvel's minion, Seth), Narga the Sea Monster and Kaymon the Gorgon Hound. They also stood against not only Malvel's human army, but Tusk the Mighty Mammoth! Malvel showed his anger by turning Seth into the final Beast Tom had to defeat – Sting the Scorpion Man! For each Beast he vanquished, Tom was gifted a precious jewel that gave him new magical powers.

And then Tom had to face a new enemy – Arax the Soul Stealer...

KAYMON

Kaymon is one of the most unusual of all the Beasts Tom has faced. A giant dog with vicious sharp teeth is deadly enough – but when that dog can split himself into three, defeating him is almost impossible.

ADURO

Aduro guides Tom through his Beast Quests. There is little the Good Wizard doesn't know about the Beasts – both good and evil. Aduro is the most powerful wizard in all the known kingdoms, and, with Marc his apprentice, works tirelessly to thwart Malvel's evil plans. His deepest regret is that, a long time ago, he accepted Malvel as his apprentice, not knowing that the young wizard harboured a dark soul.

TALADON

Tom's father, Taladon, grew up longing for adventure. After serving in Avantia's army, King Hugo made Taladon Master of the Beasts. Taladon's missions took him away from his family, and Malvel turned him into a ghost for over ten years...

THE AMULET OF AVANTIA

After returning from Gorgonia, Tom and Elenna joined King Hugo's army. Tom was stunned when a call went up across the palace: "Taladon has returned!"

But all was not as it seemed. Taladon was half-ghost! Tom vowed he would return his father to human form by reclaiming the broken Amulet of Avantia, and defeating the guardian Beasts in the Forbidden Lands! First Tom challenged Nixa the Death Bringer, Equinus the Spirit Horse and Rashouk the Cave-Troll. After each successful Quest, Tom claimed a piece of the Amulet and his father was closer to returning – but this also meant that Tom was losing the powers from the Golden Armour. Despite this, Tom journeyed fearlessly across the Forbidden Lands, meeting Luna the Moon-Wolf, Blaze the Ice-Dragon, and finally Stealth the Ghost Panther.

RASHOUK

Tom came close to failing his Beast Quest in the battle against Rashouk the Cave Troll. This Beast could turn his victims to stone with his sharp, cruel fingernails, and avoided Tom's attacks by switching to ghostly form. He was almost impossible to defeat! Almost...

THE SHADE OF DEATH

In the kingdom of Gwildor, a Dark Wizard called Velmal controlled the Good Beasts. Tom and Elenna set sail for Gwildor, but were attacked by Krabb, Master of the Sea, and Tom's hand was poisoned. Gwildor's Mistress of the Beasts, Freya, was also under Velmal's spell. Tom wrestled with Hawkite, Arrow of the Air, and Rokk the Walking Mountain. But his poisoned hand got worse every day!

In icy Freeshor, Tom stood up to Koldo the Arctic Warrior, and also crossed swords with fearsome Freya. During his next Quest, against Trema the Earth Lord, Velmal told Tom that only a relative's blood could cure his hand – but Tom had no relatives in Gwildor!

Or did he? When Tom fought Freya again, he cut her. Freya's blood splashed onto his hand and cured it. Tom was stunned – Freya was his mother!

After liberating Amictus the Bug Queen, Velmal opened a portal and dragged Freya into it. Tom did not hesitate to follow, even though he had no idea where this portal led…

KOLDO

One of Tom's trickiest Quests was his challenge to free Koldo. The mighty Beast is made of ice, and vulnerable to fire. Tom found him as a prisoner of the people of Freeshor. But once freed, Koldo became very angry, and would have destroyed the town if Tom had not stood in his way.

FREYA

Freya is Gwildor's Mistress of the Beasts, and one of the fiercest warriors in all the known kingdoms. She is also Tom's long-lost mother. Tom is excited to have her back in his life – but there are many questions to ask her, one day.

THE WORLD OF CHAOS

Tom and Elenna's next Beast Quest took them to a new kingdom, Kayonia, ruled by Queen Romaine – a realm that had been plunged into chaos. They had to save Freya from Velmal's dark magic and free Kayonia from the wrath of six terrifying Beasts.

Tom hunted Velmal all over Kayonia, battling six Beasts as he went. First was Komodo the Lizard King, then Muro the Rat Monster. Throughout his journey, Velmal taunted Tom with visions of Freya as she edged closer towards death. Tom and Elenna next fought Fang the Bat Fiend, Murk the Swamp Man, and then Terra, Curse of the Forest.

Finally, Tom's journey took him to Kayonia's capital city, Meaton, where he faced the final Beast – Vespick the Wasp Queen. After defeating Vespick, Tom liberated his mother from Velmal's magic once and for all. With their Quest complete, Tom and his companions stepped through a new portal that would take them home to Avantia.

Or so they thought...

MALVEL AND VELMAL, THE DARK WIZARDS

Tom must face Dark Wizards on his Quests. In Avantia, it is Malvel who challenges Tom. In Gwildor, it was Velmal who bent the Beasts and their guardian, Freya, to his will. Tom may not have the ability to cast spells, but he is more than a match for these two. He knows they will always return – and when they do, Tom will be ready.

FANG

Fang was one of the most dangerous of the Beasts – Tom could not get close to Fang without the Beast's magic making him blind. His battle against Fang took him to the depths of the Golden Valley, and taught Tom how to use his other senses when he could not depend on his eyes.

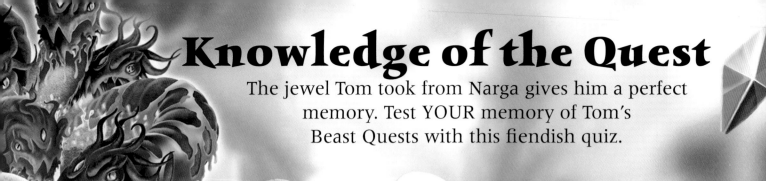

Knowledge of the Quest

The jewel Tom took from Narga gives him a perfect memory. Test YOUR memory of Tom's Beast Quests with this fiendish quiz.

SECTION 1: People of Avantia

1 Tom was raised by his Aunt Maria and Uncle Henry. What is Henry's job?
A) Farmer
B) Blacksmith
C) Medicine man

2 The wizard Aduro has an apprentice. What is his name?
A) Marc
B) Mitch
C) Martin

3 Why was the return of Tom's father Taladon spooky?
A) Because he had two heads
B) Because he was half-man, half-Beast
C) Because he was a ghost

SECTION 2: The Beasts

4 Tom's first ever Beast Quest saw him battle which Good Beast of Avantia?
A) Sepron
B) Epos
C) Ferno

5 Trillion is a three-headed lion, but which Beast is a giant dog that can split himself in three?
A) Equinus
B) Stealth
C) Kaymon

6 Which deadly Beast is known as the Soul Stealer?
A) Fang
B) Arax
C) Luna

SECTION 3: Strange Kingdoms

7 Who is Gwildor's Mistress of the Beasts?
A) Elenna
B) Freya
C) Maria

8 What is the name of the Beast who can turn people to stone?
A) Nixa
B) Soltra
C) Trema

9 Romaine is the Warrior Queen who rules which kingdom?
A) Kayonia
B) Rion
C) Gwildor

Answers can be found on pages 60-61

A BATTLE OF WITS

Beast Quests aren't always about fighting. Sometimes Tom has to think his way out of danger. Can you answer the clues below? When you've completed the grid, rearrange the letters in the shaded squares to reveal Tom's loyal friend.

Down

1 Beware this Beast's single staring eye (6)
2 Tom's compass says Destiny _ _ Danger (2)
3 The evil opposite of Aduro?   (6)
4 The _ _ _ _ _ _ _ _ _ Land is east of Avantia (9)
6 Freya is Tom's mother and _ _ _ _ _ _ _ is Tom's father (7)
9 The time between day and night, when Luna the Moon Wolf makes the wild animals attack (4)

Across

1 Beware this boy Beast and his sister, Sethrina (4)
4 Gwildor's Mistress of the Beasts (5)
5 Tom got the belt to hold his magical jewels from this Beast (6)
7 Second part of the name you find on the front of every Beast Quest book (5)
8 First part of the name you find on the front of every Beast Quest book (4)
10 Tom takes his _ _ _ _ _ and shield on every Quest (5)
11 You will find this Beast at the Stonewin volcano (4)
12 The land where two baby dragons were taken so they could grow up safely (4)

TOM'S LOYAL FRIEND IS:

__ __ __ __ __ __

Answers can be found on pages 60-61

Reptus the Ocean King

As Master of the Beasts, Taladon trains young Beasts to become Protectors of Good. He has recently returned from Rion, where he trained Vedra and Krimon, twin dragons born from the same egg. I couldn't wait to hear how the young dragons had progressed. But my father's tale involved a terrifying Beast...

"No, Krimon!" yelled Taladon, as he rode the young dragon across the sky. But it was too late – Krimon opened his jaws and sent out a jet of fire.

An apple tree burst into flame and a farmer looked up and shook his fist.

Taladon rolled his eyes. "Krimon," he said, "when will you learn that orchards aren't for target practice?"

"Some protection those dragons are!" shouted the farmer.

Krimon snorted a puff of smoke through his nostrils, roaring in welcome as Vedra emerged through clouds.

Vedra's green scales glinted as he spiralled towards them. He opened his jaws and let out a mouthful of river water onto the apple tree's smouldering branches.

"See, they're not completely hopeless," Taladon called after the farmer. Krimon soared up into the air and Vedra climbed with them. Taladon suddenly had an idea for how to deter Krimon from burning any more crops. He pointed his sword down. "Go!"

A river shimmered beneath them. Krimon was diving straight towards it. As his talons struck the water, Krimon tried to wheel away, but Taladon leant forward, guiding the dragon into the river.

"This will cool that hot head of yours," he laughed.

Krimon emerged with strands of weed stuck across him. The young dragon tossed his head, covering Taladon in water droplets.

"Hey," said Taladon. "Haven't you learnt—" But he stopped. The river was churning. Fish were struggling over each other. "They're fleeing something," Taladon realised. His gaze fell on the river-mouth. What he saw there made his blood freeze.

A fleet of black ships swept into the river. Their dark red sails hung from tall, spiked masts. A figure was silhouetted at the prow of the largest ship.

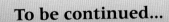

"The Pirates of Makai," said Taladon, his heart pounding. "And Sanpao, their Pirate King." Above Sanpao's head a flag whipped in the wind, bearing an emblem that showed a fearsome serpent – a Beast, long thought lost. Reptus the Ocean King. "Are the pirates in league with Reptus?" Taladon muttered.

Krimon's body shook as he gave a furious roar, which was answered by Vedra.

"You're right," Taladon shouted to the dragons. "The town is in danger. We must tell everyone to flee!" He leaned to one side to make Krimon turn. Vedra swooped towards them, his wingtips touching Krimon's.

But with a rumbling sound, the waters beneath them parted. A gigantic black and red serpent shot out of the river and crashed into the two dragons. The force of the blow nearly threw Taladon from Krimon's back. Krimon rolled through the air, beating his wings and swirling his tail to right himself. Vedra twisted himself over, his nostrils smoking.

Reptus's enormous body was as long as Sepron's, his open jaws lined with sharp red teeth. His forked tongue flickered. There was a strange, diamond-shaped dent between his glittering eyes.

Are Vedra and Krimon ready to fight Reptus? thought Taladon.

To be continued...

MAKE YOUR OWN BATTLE SWORD

Every warrior needs a trusted weapon to protect them from danger! Whenever he's in peril, Tom knows that he can rely on his sword. It is a gift from Wizard Aduro. Are you ready to arm yourself with your own precious blade?

YOU WILL NEED:
- PENCIL
- RULER
- WHITE CARDBOARD
- SCISSORS
- NEWSPAPERS
- STICKY TAPE
- KITCHEN ROLL
- TIN FOIL
- SAUCER
- PAPER GLUE
- SILVER SPRAY PAINT
- BROWN POSTER PAINT
- PAINTBRUSH
- CARD

1 Use a pencil and a ruler to draw a long blade shape onto the cardboard. Cut the blade out, then lay it back on the card and trace another identical shape. Cut that blade out, too.

2 Fold each of the blades in half very carefully, pinching a crease along the vertical centre lines.

3 Take three sheets of newspaper. Roll them into a tight tube. Trim the tube down if necessary, then tape it inside one of the blades. Lay the other blade on top and tape it in place.

4 Find a piece of card 15cm deep and roll it into a tube. Tape this around the newspaper to form a handle.

5

Cut into the middle of an old kitchen towel roll so that it can be slotted into the handle to make a hand guard. Tape it into position. If you want to shape your hand guard like Tom's, cut the ends of the rolls then tape them closed.

6

Roll some tin foil into three small balls. Push a foil ball into each end of the hand guard and the top of the handle. The shape of your sword is complete!

7

Squeeze some glue into a saucer then mix in an equal amount of water. Tear some thin strips of newspaper and put them in a pile.

8

Dip a strip of newspaper into the glue mixture, then lay it over the blade. Work your way all over the sword until the whole thing is covered with a layer of newspaper. Leave the reinforced sword to dry for at least 24 hours.

9

Cover your worktop with newspaper, then spray the entire sword with silver paint. Let the paint dry, then turn it over and respray any sections that came into contact with the worktop during the drying process.

10

Hold your silver sword by the blade and carefully paint the handle in brown poster paint. Leave the handle to dry, then take your sword by the hilt and prepare for battle!

TAKE CARE WITH SCISSORS – ASK AN ADULT TO HELP!

BRAVE COMPANIONS

Tom couldn't complete his Beast Quests without Elenna, Storm and Silver. Storm's pace means Tom can cover long distances in a short time, while Silver's keen senses sniff out danger.

But Elenna is Tom's most important companion. She can fight and use her healing skills to treat wounds. With Elenna by his side, Tom never gives up on a Quest.

Who would you take on a Beast Quest? Does your best friend or your loyal animal have what it takes? Use the space below to draw one human companion and two animal companions. Think about what useful skills they could have.

Don't forget to include yourself in the drawing, too, leading your friends on a deadly Beast Quest...

DANGER DESTINY

Ferno vs Blaze

FERNO

The first Beast Tom and Elenna ever faced, and a noble protector of Avantia. Ferno is one of Tom's most loyal friends.

AGE: 288
POWER: 212
MAGIC LEVEL: 180
FRIGHT FACTOR: 91

STRENGTHS

Ferno is one of the biggest of all Beasts. He's so huge, Tom and Elenna once mistook him for a cave. A Beast this size is extremely strong, and his fierce claws can shatter rock. But his greatest strength is his ability to breathe fire so hot it can turn trees to cinders in seconds.

WEAKNESSES

Ferno's great size can be a weakness as well as a strength. He's so big that sometimes he is not fast enough to avoid quick attacks. If his opponent could get behind him, or onto his back, would Avantia's Fire Dragon be agile enough to wrestle himself free?

TOM SAYS:

"These dragons were two of the toughest foes I've ever faced, but who would come out on top if they faced each other? Ferno's fire would be neutralised by Blaze's ice. And Blaze would be in trouble if Ferno managed to take a firm hold of him and keep him on the ground. Who do YOU think would win in this duel?"

The Beasts rarely cross paths these days, but what would happen if they did? Study the profiles of these matched Beasts, and debate with your friends who would emerge victorious in battle.

BLAZE

One of the mysterious Ghost Beasts unleashed by Malvel, Blaze is a dragon like no other – he does not breathe fire, but ice.

AGE: 313
POWER: 210
MAGIC LEVEL: 187
FRIGHT FACTOR: 90

STRENGTHS

Blaze has a long, snake-like body – this means he can wriggle free from attacks. He can also turn his body into ghost-form when faced with a superior foe. But the real danger to watch out for is his icy breath – Blaze can freeze everything in his path in an instant.

And the winner is…

WEAKNESSES

Heat – if exposed to flame or molten lava, Blaze is unable to use his ghostly form, meaning that an opponent can strike him freely. One of the best ways to beat him is to find a way to keep him on the ground. Blaze is a true creature of the sky, and on land he becomes less agile.

23

GOOD AND EVIL: WHICH SIDE ARE YOU ON?

In Avantia, the forces of good and evil are finely balanced. Tom fights alongside Aduro and King Hugo to keep Malvel's wickedness at bay. But which side would you be on? Answer the questions to discover if you would stand up for good – or bring evil into the kingdom…

WIZARD'S STAFF
In a battle of wits, Malvel asks if you would prefer to be brave or cunning. Which do you choose?

BRAVE
You wound your opponent in a duel. **Do you:** Keep attacking! **OR** Stop fighting – your opponent needs a healer?

CUNNING
The Winding River is flooded! **Do you:** Call on Sepron to drive back the waters? **OR** Set out in a boat to rescue people?

KEEP ATTACKING
Your opponent begs you for mercy. **Do you:** Blast them with evil magic? **OR** Run them through with your blade?

STOP FIGHTING
Another soldier attacks your wounded opponent. **Do you:** Defend him with your sword? **OR** Magic a protective shield around him?

CALL ON SEPRON
Avantia's neighbour, Rion, is being attacked. **Do you:** Ignore it – let Rion fight its own battles? **OR** Go to Rion's aid?

SET OUT IN A BOAT
Malvel says he will make you king of Avantia if you fight for him. **Do you:** Turn him down? **OR** Accept, and enjoy the riches?

- BLAST WITH DARK MAGIC
- RUN THROUGH WITH YOUR BLADE
- MAGIC A PROTECTIVE SHIELD
- USE YOUR SWORD
- IGNORE RION'S CALL
- GO TO RION'S AID
- ACCEPT MALVEL'S OFFER
- TURN MALVEL DOWN

Evil Wizard

You are a true heir to Malvel! The Dark Wizard has selected you for training, and you have proved a talented and wicked pupil. If you continue down your dark path, don't be surprised if you find Tom standing in your way.

Brave Quester

You are noble and courageous, with a true heart. You have fought to defend Avantia, but also shown mercy to the kingdom's enemies. King Hugo thinks you would make a courageous companion to Tom.

START
Which weapon would you choose: a wizard's staff or a warrior's sword?

WARRIOR'S SWORD
Ferno needs help. Tom asks you to go to the Southern Caves with him. But Elenna asks for your assistance in tracking the Dark Wizard. Who will you help?

ELENNA
An evil Beast is attacking Avantia! **Do you:**
Immediately ride to the scene?
OR Go to King Hugo for advice?

TOM
Taladon has asked you to defend Avantia while he's away. **Do you:**
Replace him as Master of the Beasts – you're the better warrior? **OR** Keep the kingdom safe and step aside on his return?

RIDE TO THE SCENE
Do you use the evil Beast to attack your enemies?
OR Do you try to drive it from the kingdom?

GO TO KING HUGO FOR ADVICE
King Hugo tells you that the Beast is not evil – it's under a spell. **Do you:**
Destroy it anyway?
OR Try to free it?

REPLACE TALADON
You capture Storm and Silver! **Do you:**
Train them to attack the people of Avantia? **OR** Cast a spell to make them sleep forever?

KEEP THE KINGDOM SAFE
Malvel sends an evil Beast to attack the Palace. **Do you:**
Raise an army to defend it? **OR** Blast the Beast with your magic?

DRIVE IT FROM THE KINGDOM

ATTACK YOUR ENEMIES

TRY TO FREE IT

DESTROY IT

CAST A SLEEPING SPELL

TRAIN THEM TO ATTACK

RAISE AN ARMY

BLAST WITH MAGIC

Evil Warrior

Seth admires your cunning and treachery – together, you could destroy Avantia! You're an excellent sword-fighter too, but your real skill is fighting with a spiked metal ball on a chain. Your wicked deeds mean you have many enemies across the kingdom.

Good Wizard

Avantia's future depends on you – and your incredible skill with magic. Aduro has taught you his most secret magical knowledge, and you've used it to invent a new protective spell. Your fighting skills are impressive, too.

25

Epos's CHOCOLATE LAVA CAKES

These cakes are filled with oozy molten chocolate centres and topped with red strawberry lava. Those that eat them feel an instant connection with Epos, the great Phoenix.

To make a cake each for yourself and a party of seven favoured companions, you will need:

- 200g unsalted butter, plus extra for greasing
- 200g dark chocolate
- 1 teaspoon of vanilla extract
- 8 teaspoons of granulated sugar
- 4 whole eggs and 4 extra yolks
- 110g caster sugar
- 60g plain flour
- A pinch of salt
- Strawberry ice cream sauce

KITCHENS CAN BE DANGEROUS! ALWAYS ASK AN ADULT BEFORE YOU GET STARTED.

1 Ask an adult to pre-heat the oven to 230°C/450°F/Gas Mark 8. Fill a small saucepan with 5cm of water, then simmer on the hob. Place a heat-safe glass bowl on top of the pan. Drop in the chocolate and butter. When the ingredients are both melted, stir in the vanilla extract.

2 Put the chocolate mixture on one side to cool, then set out eight individual mini pie dishes on a baking tray. Use a sheet of kitchen towel dipped in butter to rub the inside of each of the dishes. Evenly sprinkle one teaspoon of granulated sugar inside each one.

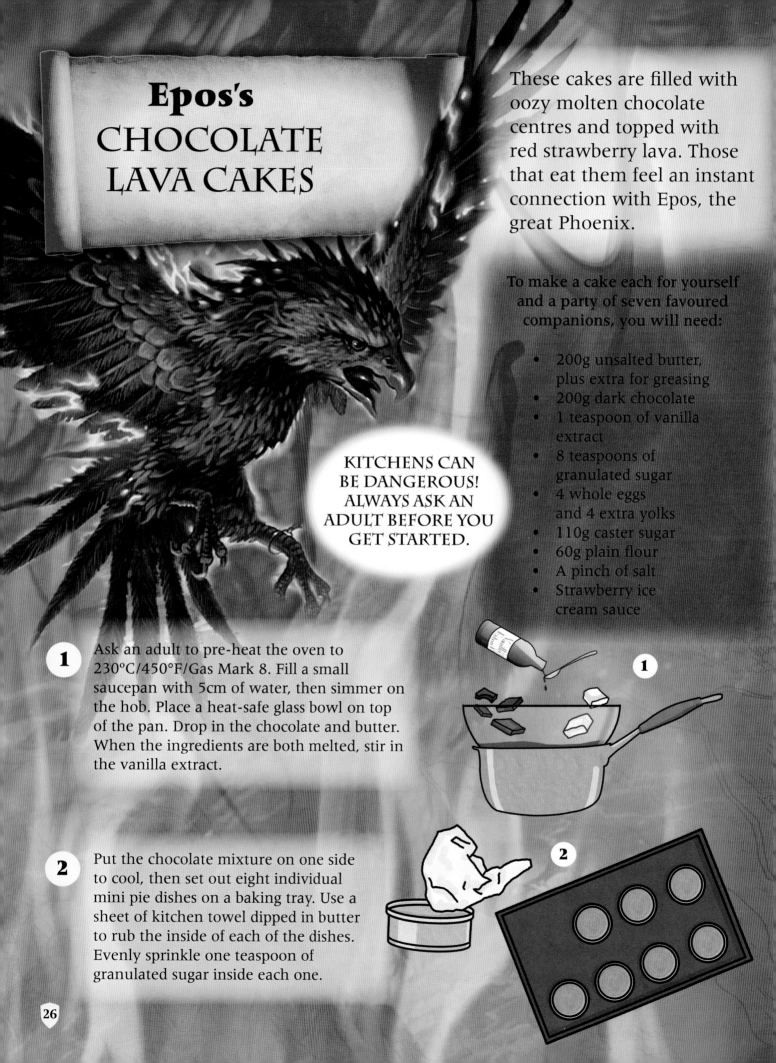

3 Take an egg and ask an adult to help you separate the white from the yolk. Repeat this three times. Tip the 4 yolks into a large mixing bowl, then crack in the whole eggs too. Beat them together using an electric whisk, slowly tipping in the caster sugar. The mixture should magically puff up in size!

4 Gently fold in the melted chocolate mixture next, followed by the flour and a pinch of salt.

5 Carefully spoon your gooey mixture into the dishes so that they're all equally filled. Put them in the middle of the oven for 12 minutes, until the top is very slightly domed but not fully risen.

6 Put the cakes on the side to cool for a few minutes, then round up your friends! Run a knife around the inside of each pie dish to loosen the lava cake, then place a tea plate against it. Quickly flip the plate over and lift the dish off so that the cake stands on its own.

7 Serve up all the cakes, then splatter each one with a spray of strawberry ice cream sauce – the more lava the better! Now dig a fork into your mini-volcano and watch the oozy chocolate lava spill out.

Lava Cakes need to be eaten warm – don't make this recipe until you're hungry!

CREATE YOUR OWN REALM

Tom's Beast Quests have taken him to lands far from Avantia. He's seen kingdoms such as Rion, Gorgonia, Gwildor and Kayonia. Now he must journey to a new realm: yours!

IDEAS

BEASTS
CASTLE
DESERT
FARMLAND
FORESTS
GRASSY PLAINS
ICY PLAINS
LAKES
MARSHES
PALACE
QUICKSAND
RAINFORESTS
RIVERS
TOWNS
VILLAGES
VOLCANOES
WOODS

Fill in the space to create your own realm. You could choose your favourite Beasts and decide where they live, or invent new Beasts. Think up a name for your realm and decide what kind of ruler you are – a king, queen, or even a wizard.

THE REALM OF

....

RULED BY

....

Reptus the Ocean King…
continued

Reptus's forked tail rose out of the river and lashed at the smouldering orchard. Villagers ran from the Beast, screaming in terror.

"Go, young dragons!" Taladon yelled. The twin dragons swooped, breathing fiery streams at Reptus, but the Ocean King sank out of sight.

Taladon heard the water breaking again, followed by Reptus's furious roar. The Beast was behind them!

"Up!" Taladon commanded, pulling on Krimon's scales as Reptus's teeth snapped at his tail. Krimon and Vedra soared out of reach. Below, Reptus hissed angrily. Taladon considered their next move. Vedra and Krimon were still young and their fire wasn't yet powerful enough to do damage from great distances.

"But I can't bring them close," Taladon muttered. "Reptus is too deadly…"

Down below, Reptus turned towards the orchard. He had seen something...

Taladon urged Krimon a little lower, using the power of the Golden Helmet to see deep into the orchard. Now he could spot what Reptus was looking at.

"Oh no," Taladon breathed. An elderly farm worker sat astride a mule pulling an empty cart. The old man tried vainly to control his animal as it bucked at the sounds coming from the river. One of the cart's wheels was stuck in a tree root.

They were trapped!

"Down!" Taladon called, guiding Krimon towards the orchard, just as Reptus jabbed his long neck over the riverbank. His cruel red teeth latched onto the cart, pulling it free and dragging it towards the water.

"Help!" cried the old man as he tried to spur his frightened mule forward. "Somebody help!"

As Krimon got closer to the ground, Taladon stood up. He called on the power of his Golden Boots to somersault over the trees. He landed two horse-lengths from the cart, which was almost in the water.

"Hold the reins tight!" Taladon called to the old man as he bounded forward. He grabbed the frayed rope connecting the cart to the mule's saddle. He pulled on the rope, his magical strength from the Golden Breastplate more than a match for Reptus. The Beast tugged at the cart but couldn't move it.

"Thank you, brave knight!" the old man gasped. Above, Vedra and Krimon circled, distracting Reptus.

"Is your mule fast of foot?" Taladon asked.

"Not really," said the elderly farm worker, "but he'll find speed enough to flee this monster!"

One of the dragon twins sent a jet of fire into the Beast's face but he ducked out of the way, turning back to stare again at Taladon. Reptus was not done with him. Taladon unsheathed his sword and severed the rope that held the cart. Taken by surprise, Reptus's head lashed back, dragging the empty cart into the river.

Taladon slapped the mule's flank. "Be gone!" he called. The man and his mule galloped away.

But Reptus wasn't defeated. The terrifying Beast rose to his full height, poised to strike.

Taladon stood firm, sword held ready. But Reptus suddenly froze. The diamond-shaped dent between the Beast's eyes shone with a dull, red glow that pulsed.

He's listening to something, Taladon realised. But what?

Reptus turned towards the river-mouth.

Following the Beast's gaze, Taladon saw the fleet of pirate ships. He squinted at the figure on the prow of the first ship – Sanpao, the Pirate King. He had his left hand held in front of his mouth, and grasped a diamond – the same size and shape as the curious dent in Reptus's head. *He's talking into the diamond*, Taladon realised, as Sanpao's free hand pointed towards the river's bank. *Reptus is receiving orders!*

To be continued...

The Beast Gauntlet

Malvel once wore the Beast Gauntlet to control the six Good Beasts of Avantia, but he lost it when Tom freed them. Now, the Gauntlet has reappeared!

Can you help Tom reach the Beast Gauntlet before the Dark Wizard does?

HOW TO PLAY

You will need a dice, plus a counter for each player. Place your counters on the start shield, then decide who's going first. Roll the dice to see how many spaces you can move. Good luck…

START

You hide from Torgor the Minotaur. Miss a turn.

Malvel has spotted you. Go back one space.

Ferno the Fire Dragon gives you a ride. Go forward five spaces.

Aduro comes to your aid. Roll again.

King Hugo sends you a good luck message. Go forward three spaces.

Trillion the Three-Headed Lion chases you. Back three spaces.

Ask Epos the Flame Bird to carry a player of your choice back to the START.

You're surrounded by hyenas! Go back four spaces.

Storm's horseshoe needs replacing. Miss a turn.

Silver hunts some rabbits for you to eat. Roll again.

FINISH

You reach into the tree branches and seize the Beast Gauntlet. Avantia is safe!

Taladon gives you some sword-fighting advice. Go forward one space.

Rashouk the Cave Troll grabs you and drops you back seven spaces.

Elenna joins your Quest. Go forward four spaces.

Malvel blasts you aside. Miss a turn.

Malvel uses his Dark Magic to create a fog, and you get lost. Miss a turn.

You reach up to grab the Beast Gauntlet, but fall to the ground. Go back one space.

You eat the supplies Aunt Maria gave you. Go forward three spaces.

DANGER ~ DESTINY

MALVEL'S QUIZ

On his Beast Quests, Tom must learn everything he can about the kingdom and the Beasts he battles. But he must find out about his enemies, too – only then will he be able to defeat them. Test your knowledge of the Dark Wizard Malvel...

1 **What is the name of the kingdom that Malvel rules?**

A) Gorgonia
B) Gwildor
C) Kayonia

2 **Which Good Wizard was Malvel's teacher?**

A) Jonah
B) Aduro
C) Marc

3 **After Tom defeated Malvel by releasing the Good Beasts of Avantia from his magic, what magical artefact did Malvel steal from the Palace?**

A) The Golden Armour
B) Aduro's spell book
C) Tom's shield

4 **What is the name of Seth's sister?**
A) Serena
B) Selena
C) Sethrina

5 **How did Malvel punish Seth for failing to defeat Tom?**

A) He turned him into a cockroach
B) He shrank him to the size of a rat
C) He transformed him into a Beast

Answers can be found on pages 60-61

TOM'S QUEST MEMORIES

These are some of Tom's most memorable moments from his Beast Quests. What are YOUR favourite Beast Quest moments?

1
Sepron
"My very first Quest at sea! I'm glad Sepron is now my great friend."

2
Kragos & Kildor
"Elenna and I have faced Beasts with two heads before – but never a Two-Headed Demon!"

3
Nixa
"This Beast shape-shifted into an exact copy of Elenna, and almost had me fooled!"

4
Amictus
"For this Quest we were in a sweltering jungle, battling a Bug Queen who had hundreds of young to attack us."

5
Vipero
"This giant, two-headed Snake-Man was very hard to beat, especially in the scorching heat of the desert!"

MY TOP 5 FAVOURITE BEAST QUESTS

1 ....
2 ....
3 ....
4 ....
5 ....

SPOT THE IMPOSTER!

Fearsome Nixa the Death Bringer is a shape shifter, and can take the form of any person or Beast. Look closely at these two pictures of King Hugo. One of these is the real king, and one is Nixa in disguise. Can you spot the five clues that reveal the impostor?

Answers can be found on pages 60-61

CROSS THE ICY PATH

Can you help Tom pass by Blaze the Ice Dragon, without being struck by his deadly ice? Look carefully at the path until you find a word that will lead him to the other side.

Answers can be found on pages 60-61

Krabb vs Narga

KRABB

Gwildor's Master of the Sea infected Tom with a deadly poison that almost cost him his right hand. Luckily, Tom was able to release him from Velmal's enchantment.

AGE: 261
POWER: 190
MAGIC LEVEL: 184
FRIGHT FACTOR: 88

STRENGTHS

Krabb has eight long legs that enable him to launch simultaneous attacks from different angles. They also make him a very fast swimmer. His vicious pincers are sharp enough to chop sharks in half, and he is as comfortable fighting above the surface as he is underwater.

WEAKNESSES

Krabb is vulnerable to attacks from above or behind, where his legs and pincers cannot reach. These legs and pincers are perhaps too long for their own good – if an opponent avoids Krabb's strikes and gets in close, Gwildor's noble Beast struggles to defend himself.

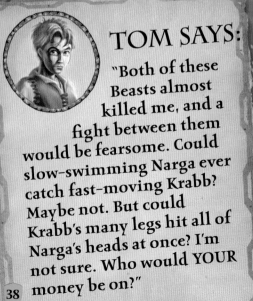

TOM SAYS:

"Both of these Beasts almost killed me, and a fight between them would be fearsome. Could slow-swimming Narga ever catch fast-moving Krabb? Maybe not. But could Krabb's many legs hit all of Narga's heads at once? I'm not sure. Who would YOUR money be on?"

The most difficult Quests Tom faces are those at sea! But in an ocean battle between these two great Beasts, who would emerge victorious?

AGE: 346
POWER: 233
MAGIC LEVEL: 146
FRIGHT FACTOR: 87

NARGA

Gorgonia's Sea Monster is the scourge of the kingdom's rebels: a hideous Beast who devours people and ships alike.

STRENGTHS

Narga has six heads that can strike from different angles simultaneously; their combined strength means that Narga can lift and throw even the sturdiest of ships. His bulbous body is so large that sea-farers mistake it for dangerous rocks.

And the winner is...

WEAKNESSES

Narga can sometimes be too eager to attack and destroy, causing his many heads to collide and his necks to become entangled. His size prevents him from hiding in shallow waters, and makes him a slow swimmer.

ELENNA'S HEALING POWERS

Elenna uses her knowledge of herbs and remedies to heal cuts and relieve sickness. Can you fit these ingredients vertically into the grid below to help Elenna mix up a healing potion?

NETTLE   PEPPERCORN   SNAIL
TOOTH   DANDELION   ACORNS

P O T I O N

Answers can be found on pages 60-61

A Scene to Remember...

To succeed on a Beast Quest, Tom must remain alert at all times! Study the scene below for ten seconds, then turn over the page and see if you can answer all the questions correctly.

Test Your Memory!

1. How many wasps are there in the picture?
2. What colour are the cat-Beast's eyes?
3. What is Tom holding in his right hand?
4. How many planets are there in the sky?
5. Which Beast is on top of the tower?
6. What is sticking out of the pile of Beast dung?

Answers can be found on pages 60-61

MALVEL'S MAZE

A Beast Quest isn't just about battling Beasts – Tom also has to deal with Wizard Malvel's evil magic! Help Tom find his way through the maze below. You must avoid the Beasts, or Tom's Quest will be over...

Answers can be found on pages 60-61

GROW A DARK JUNGLE

Tom will never forget his time in the Dark Jungle. It was there that he encountered Claw the Giant Monkey! The Jungle is suffocatingly hot, with danger lurking behind every vine. This page will reveal the secret of creating a tropical forest of your very own.

You will need:
A jumbo-sized empty squash bottle
Scissors
A few handfuls of sand
A few handfuls of compost
Some African violets or ferns
Some small rocks
Water
Sticky tape

1

Ask an adult to cut off the top third of the bottle and set it to one side.

2

Fill the bottom of the bottle with a layer of sand. Now top the sand with compost, up to a third of the height of the bottle.

3

Use your fingers to push holes into the soil, then gently ease your plants into the bottle. Put some rocks in amongst the foliage.

4

Give your jungle some water, then rest the bottle lid back on the top again. Wind the sticky tape around the bottle, making sure that no air can get in.

5

Place your bottle in a sunny place and watch it grow! Your Dark Jungle will water itself, but if the plants start to wilt, move it out of direct sunlight.

The plants in your Dark Jungle will water themselves for weeks by taking moisture up from the soil and circulating it around the bottle! Every month, unscrew the squash lid and spritz a little more water in to keep your forest alive.

Always ask an adult before using sharp scissors!

A Hero's Powers

There are two things Tom could not do without on his Beast Quests. The first is his best friend, Elenna, and the second is his magical tokens. These tokens give him increased ability to do battle with the Beasts.

THE SHIELD

After liberating Ferno the Fire Dragon from Malvel's evil spell, Tom was rewarded with a dragon scale. The scale slotted into his shield and now the shield could protect him from fire. With each Beast he freed, Tom collected another token and another magical power.

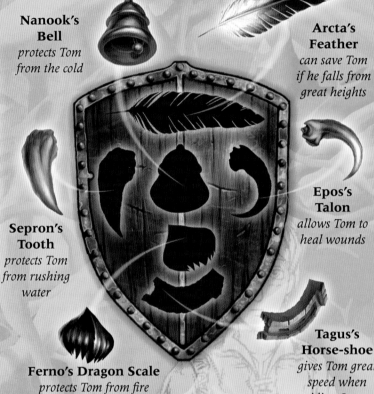

Nanook's Bell
protects Tom from the cold

Arcta's Feather
can save Tom if he falls from great heights

Sepron's Tooth
protects Tom from rushing water

Epos's Talon
allows Tom to heal wounds

Ferno's Dragon Scale
protects Tom from fire

Tagus's Horse-shoe
gives Tom great speed when riding Storm

THE JEWELLED BELT

On his Quest to Gorgonia, Tom battled six terrifying Beasts. After Torgor the Minotaur was defeated, the Beast's belt appeared around Tom's waist. After vanquishing the Dark Beasts, six jewels appeared in the belt.

Torgor's Red Jewel
gives Tom the ability to understand what the Beasts think and feel

Kaymon's White Jewel
allows Tom to send his shadow ahead to check for danger

Sting's Purple Jewel
gives Tom the strength to cut through stone with his sword.

Skor's Green Jewel
enables Tom to mend broken bones

Narga's Yellow Jewel
provides Tom with a perfect memory

Tusk's Amber Jewel
sharpens Tom's sword skills

THE GOLDEN ARMOUR

On his second Beast Quest, Tom collected pieces of the Golden Armour. Each piece gave Tom a new magical power. But the armour did not belong to Tom. It belonged to the real Master of the Beasts – Tom's father, Taladon. And Taladon soon reclaimed the six pieces of armour, along with their magical powers. But one day, the title of Master of the Beasts and the armour will pass on to Tom...

45

Colours of Gwildor

One of Tom's most unusual Beast Quests took him to Gwildor, twin kingdom of Avantia. During this Quest, Tom battled Hawkite, Arrow of the Air. Use the grid below to copy the outline of Hawkite, then colour her in.

ELENNA'S WARNING!

Elenna needs your help! Tom is on a vital Beast Quest to a dark corner of Avantia, and she has to send him an urgent message. But Malvel has struck her with one of his evil spells, and all of her words are jumbled up! Can you unscramble her warning?

EB RECFUAL!
LEVLAM SHA STE A
PART ORF UYO!

___ _____!

_____ ___ ___ ___ __

____ ___ ___!

Answers can be found on pages 60-61

DRAW YOUR OWN BEAST QUEST

Tom has had many spectacular battles against terrifying Beasts. Here, you will have the chance to draw your own version of one of his greatest Quests – against Zepha the Monster Squid. Use a pencil to fill in the blank panels, and tell the story of Tom versus Zepha in your own way!

1

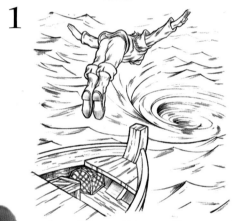

The only way Tom could tackle Zepha the Monster Squid was by facing the Beast in its own lair…underwater!

2

The whirlpool was strong and fierce, but soon Tom felt a sharp rock on the sea floor. He clung to it, and saw…the Golden Helmet!

3

But before Tom could reach the Golden Helmet, Zepha arrived! And the Beast was angry…

4

Tom tried to swim for safety, but his lungs started to hurt as Zepha chased him. He had to breathe soon, or he would die!

5

After coming up for air, Tom dived back into the water with his sword and shield - he was determined to defeat this Beast.

6

But even Tom's sword couldn't finish off Zepha. Was all lost? No, because Sepron arrived to help Tom out!

7

Tom used his sword against Zepha, while Sepron wrapped the squid up tightly in his coils.

8

Tom watched, amazed, as Zepha's body exploded, turning into thousands of tiny squid that swam away in fear. The Beast was defeated!

Reptus the Ocean King
The Final Chapter

The pirate ship had almost reached Horton. Taladon could see Sanpao clearly now. The front of his scalp was shaven, and the rest of his hair was coiled in a long braid. Darts were embedded in the thick plait. The Pirate King spoke into the diamond he held, looking up at Reptus.

"What evil has Sanpao commanded now?" Taladon muttered.

The Beast rose up in the river, his forked tail beating the water.

"Vedra! Krimon!" Taladon yelled. He gestured with his sword towards the pirate fleet. "Attack!"

With a roar, Vedra and Krimon dived towards the ships. Taladon saw Vedra tearing away the flag from Sanpao's vessel. Krimon swooped down, knocking many pirates off their feet.

The Ocean King lunged at Taladon. He rolled aside, and the Beast's massive head smashed a rock. Reptus turned back towards the fleet, and Taladon saw that Sanpao was talking into the diamond again. *I must take the diamond from Sanpao and control Reptus myself*, he realised.

He sprinted up a rocky outcrop. As he ran, Taladon bellowed at Vedra and Krimon. They swerved away from the pirate ships and flew down. Just as Reptus thrust his head forwards, Vedra swooped. Taladon leapt onto the green dragon's back and Reptus's jaws snapped closed on empty air.

"Up!" yelled Taladon. He gripped Vedra's flanks, directing the dragons towards Sanpao's ship. As the red sails loomed towards him, Taladon jumped.

He landed on the deck. The pirates surrounded him. Taladon's blade clashed against their cutlasses.

"Stand aside," snarled a voice.

The pirates parted to reveal Sanpao. The diamond hung about his neck.

"Taladon the Swift," Sanpao continued. "We meet again."

"Call Reptus away from Horton," Taladon growled.

"Not until we've taken every last coin," Sanpao snarled, reaching for another throwing dart – this was Taladon's chance! He swung his sword through the cord that held the diamond. Taladon struck Sanpao's temple with the hilt of his weapon. As the Pirate King fell to the deck, Taladon stooped to catch the stone. He brought the diamond to his lips. "Reptus," he bellowed, "I command you to destroy this evil fleet!"

Reptus slithered into the water. Sanpao pulled himself to his feet, eyes wide with fear as the Beast approached.

"That's right," Taladon yelled. "Reptus has switched sides."

Reptus began to destroy the fleet and the ships sank. Taladon was dragged underwater.

The force of the water prised his sword and the diamond from his hands. *I can only reach one of them*, Taladon realised. *I don't have time to rescue both.*

He grabbed his sword. Taladon spotted Krimon's red scales glimmering above the water. He kicked upwards, reaching towards the young dragon as the diamond sank into the depths.

"That was close!" he gasped, bursting through the water. But the powerful diamond was lost...for ever?

Sanpao and his men left Rion after the battle, but I'm sure their greed will bring them back. My father believes the diamond still lies in the riverbed. Perhaps one day it will be found. But will Reptus's new master be good or evil...?

Tagus vs Sting

TAGUS

The valiant Horse-Man of Avantia's Central Plains, Tagus is a guardian of wildlife. He may look terrifying, but his heart is on the side of Good.

AGE: 406
POWER: 73
MAGIC LEVEL: 114
FRIGHT FACTOR: 58

STRENGTHS

Tagus is one of Avantia's most versatile Beasts. His human body is muscular and quick. In close-quarter combat, he can wrestle with an opponent, or fend them off with his superior swordsmanship. And his horse's legs are faster than even the fastest stallion.

WEAKNESSES

As skilled as he is, Tagus is the smallest of Avantia's Beasts, and vulnerable to attacks from the air. He is also at risk from long-range strikes - there is very little he can do to defend against dragon fire, for example. If his horse body is mounted, Tagus can be controlled by a determined rider.

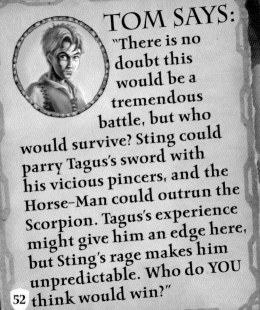

TOM SAYS:

"There is no doubt this would be a tremendous battle, but who would survive? Sting could parry Tagus's sword with his vicious pincers, and the Horse-Man could outrun the Scorpion. Tagus's experience might give him an edge here, but Sting's rage makes him unpredictable. Who do YOU think would win?"

You've pitted dragon against dragon, and sea Beast against sea Beast. But what would happen if these two Beasts of the land met in combat?

AGE: 15
POWER: 248
MAGIC LEVEL: 162
FRIGHT FACTOR: 71

STING

Gorgonia's Scorpion Man was once the boy Seth, Tom's arch-nemesis. Cursed by Malvel to live the rest of his life as a hideous Beast, Sting's anger makes him a ferocious opponent.

STRENGTHS

Sting's six spindly legs make him very fast on the ground, and his poisonous tail and two cruel pincers are deadly weapons. He is angry at being turned into a Beast, and this rage fuels his strength when attacking.

And the winner is…

WEAKNESSES

Sting has not been a Beast for very long, so has not yet mastered his powers. This means he can be outsmarted by a more experienced opponent. Although he is angry at being a Beast, the Scorpion Man is also sad that Malvel transformed him into a monster, and will sometimes lose the will to fight…

Make Your Own Ferno

Now that Ferno is free from Malvel's curse, he protects the homesteads along the Winding River. And he can protect you, too! Hang this magnificent dragon in your room and it will guard you all night long.

YOU WILL NEED:

Thin card in black, blue, red and white
Ruler
Pencil
Paper glue
Scissors
Black felt-tip pen
2 long strips of black and blue card, measuring 100cm long and 4cm wide
Silver pen

1 Use your pencil and ruler to draw a square 10cm wide on a sheet of blue card. Draw a dragon's head shape on the square and cut it out.

2 Cut four spine shapes out of card and glue these around the top of Ferno's head. Add some smaller crests above the Beast's eyes.

3 Cut some sharp white teeth out of card and stick these at the bottom of the face shape. Using a black felt-tip pen, draw the outlines of two eyes on the red card.

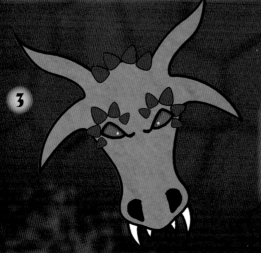

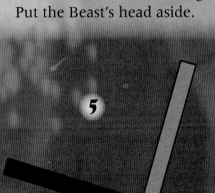

4 Using the black felt-tip pen, draw on two nostrils. Use your black pen to add extra details to the face and bring Ferno to life. Put the Beast's head aside.

5

5 Glue the end of the blue strip of card to the end of the black strip of card so the pieces are lying at right angles.

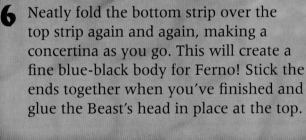

6 Neatly fold the bottom strip over the top strip again and again, making a concertina as you go. This will create a fine blue-black body for Ferno! Stick the ends together when you've finished and glue the Beast's head in place at the top.

6

7 Cut two wing shapes out of black card and a pointy arrow-head tail. Cut the pieces out, then use a silver pen to cover them in tiny scales.

7

8

8 Stick the wing shapes to the back of the dragon's head, then attach the tail to the end of his concertina body. Now Ferno is ready to guard your domain!

ALWAYS ASK AN ADULT BEFORE USING SCISSORS.

Elenna's Guide to Tracking and Trailing

Tracking and trailing means using the signs left by people and animals so you can follow them. These skills are vital on every Beast Quest!

Always ask an adult to come with you to find a Beast!

Footprints

Following a trail of prints is the easiest way to find a person, animal or Beast. What the prints look like can tell you a lot about their owner. Do they have claws? Do they have two legs, four legs – or even more?

ELENNA'S TIP

If some of the prints in the same trail look different, you're probably tracking a four-legged creature. Silver's front paws leave different marks to his back paws. This is usually the case for cats and dogs, too.

Signs of Feeding

Animals and Beasts don't always leave footprints on the ground. Some of them can fly or climb through the trees of a forest or jungle. But they will still leave a trail that you can follow. Look for signs of feeding. Are there any trees that seem to be missing fruits or nuts?

Disturbances

In the Quest against Luna the Moon Wolf, Elenna and Tom saw branches cracked and grass downtrodden by the wild creatures fleeing the Beast. This gave them an idea of just how ferocious Luna was.

Other Creatures

If a large animal or Beast is in a forest, smaller creatures are usually spooked and will want to get as far away as possible! When Tom and Elenna were looking for Trillion the Three-Headed Lion, they knew they were facing a fearsome Beast because even the hyenas were running away from their usual hunting ground.

ELENNA'S TIP

When I'm hunting in the woods with my bow and arrow, I often come across pellets. These are tiny parcels vomited up by birds such as owls and hawks. They contain bones, feathers, beaks and claws – any part of the bird's meal that it can't digest. Once I found an owl pellet that contained the whole skeleton of a mouse!

Moulting

If you have a pet cat or dog, you'll notice that they leave fur wherever they sit or sleep. This is called 'moulting'. Beasts moult too. Be on the lookout for hair, fur and feathers on the ground – these are usually good indicators of which direction the Beast is heading. But practise with your pets at home first, before you go out looking for Beasts!

Droppings

You can tell a lot about an animal or Beast by the droppings it leaves. Herbivores (plant-eaters) leave material such as grass, seeds and berries in their droppings. The dung of carnivores (meat-eaters) often includes hair and bones from the creatures they have eaten.

Malvel's Spell Room

"My friend, you have reached the end of your Beast Quest. You are in Malvel's Spell Room, where he has Freya held captive!

Did you find the six magical tokens? You need them now. They are my mother's Gwildorian Prizes, and hold her powers. She can only be freed if you put them in Malvel's cauldron..."

List the six magical tokens in the bubbles. If you haven't found them all, don't worry – there is just enough time for you to race back through the annual and hunt for the last ones...

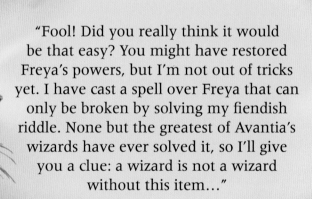

"Fool! Did you really think it would be that easy? You might have restored Freya's powers, but I'm not out of tricks yet. I have cast a spell over Freya that can only be broken by solving my fiendish riddle. None but the greatest of Avantia's wizards have ever solved it, so I'll give you a clue: a wizard is not a wizard without this item..."

My body is pale, my spine is stiff –
Only the few can receive my gifts.

My life can be long, but also brief,
And I need your help to turn a new leaf.

What am I?

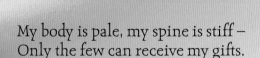

Farewell, Friend!

Your Beast Quest is complete!

Thanks to you, Freya's powers are restored and Malvel is defeated.

You are a brave and noble warrior and it has been an honour to fight alongside you. New Beasts and challenges await. Elenna, Storm, Silver and I will call on your incredible skills again.

I know that you will defend Avantia as long as there is blood in your veins.

Farewell for now, but we will meet again...

Tom

Answers

Page 14

Knowledge of the Quest

Question 1: B
Question 2: A
Question 3: C
Question 4: C
Question 5: C
Question 6: B
Question 7: B
Question 8: B
Question 9: A

Page 15

A Battle of Wits

S	E	T	H				O			M
O					F	R	E	Y	A	A
L					O					L
T	O	R	G	O	R		T			V
R					B	L	A	D	E	E
A	D	A	M		I		L			L
	U				D		A			
	S	W	O	R	D		D			
	K				E	P	O	S		
		R	I	O	N		N			

Tom's loyal friend is: Elenna

Page 34

Malvel's Quiz

Question 1: A
Question 2: B
Question 3: A
Question 4: C
Question 5: C

Page 36

Spot the Imposter

The top picture is the real King Hugo! The five changes to the bottom picture are:

(1) His pendant is blue
(2) His beard is grey
(3) His cloak is purple and red
(4) There is a red jewel at the front of his crown
(5) His left sleeve is blue.

60

Page 37
Cross the Icy Path!

Tom must cross the path by spelling out the word 'AVANTIA'.

Page 40
Elenna's healing powers

	P	N	S		
E	T	E	N	A	D
P	O	T	A	C	A
P	**O**	**T**	**I**	**O**	**N**
E	T	L	L	R	D
R	H	E		N	E
C				S	L
O					I
R					O
N					N

Page 41-42
Test Your Memory!

1. Five
2. Green
3. A sword
4. Two
5. Arachnid, the King of Spiders
6. The bones from a human arm and hand!

Page 43
Malvel's Maze

Page 47
Elenna's Warning

Elenna's warning says: BE CAREFUL! MALVEL HAS SET A TRAP FOR YOU!

Page 58
Malvel's Spellroom

The five items are hidden on the following pages:
The ring – page 12
The telescope – page 20
The pearl – page 27
The mirror – page 45
The scales – page 52
The gloves – page 57

The answer to Malvel's riddle is: A SPELL BOOK

Join the Tribe, Join the Quest

THE GOLDEN ARMOUR

978 1 84616 483 5   978 1 84616 482 8   978 1 84616 484 2   978 1 84616 988 5   978 1 84616 989 2   978 1 84616 990 8

978 1 84616 486 6   978 1 84616 485 9   978 1 84616 487 3   978 1 84616 991 5   978 1 84616 992 2   978 1 84616 993 9

THE DARK REALM   THE AMULET OF AVANTIA

978 1 84616 997 7   978 1 84616 998 4   978 1 40830 000 8   978 1 40830 376 4   978 1 40830 377 1   978 1 40830 378 8

978 1 40830 001 5   978 1 40830 002 2   978 1 40830 003 9   978 1 40830 379 5   978 1 40830 381 8   978 1 40830 380 1

THE SHADE OF DEATH   NEW SERIES! THE WORLD OF CHAOS

978 1 40830 437 2   978 1 40830 438 9   978 1 40830 439 6   978 1 40830 725 0   978 1 40830 723 6   978 1 40830 726 7

978 1 40830 440 2   978 1 40830 441 9   978 1 40830 442 6   978 1 40830 724 3   978 1 40830 727 4   978 1 40830 728 1

COMING SOON! NEW BEAST QUEST SERIES: THE LOST WORLD